# Gideon & Otto

## Olivier Dunrea

HOUGHTON MIFFLIN HARCOURT
Boston   New York

**To access the read-along audio, visit**
**WWW.HMHBOOKS.COM/FREEDOWNLOADS**
**ACCESS CODE: LOSTANDFOUND**

| AGES | GRADES | GUIDED READING LEVEL | READING RECOVERY LEVEL | LEXILE® LEVEL |
|------|--------|---------------------|------------------------|---------------|
| 4–6 | 1 | E | 7–8 | 280L |

The text of this book is set in Shannon.
The illustrations are ink and watercolor on paper.

The Library of Congress Cataloging-in-Publication Data is on file.

ISBN: 978-0-618-43662-0 hardcover
ISBN: 978-0-547-98398-1 board book
ISBN: 978-0-544-43060-0 paper over board reader
ISBN: 978-0-544-43061-7 paperback reader

Manufactured in China
SCP 10 9 8 7 6 5 4 3 2 1
4500513632

*For Amy, of course!*

This is Gideon.
Gideon is a small, ruddy gosling

This is Otto.
Otto is Gideon's favorite friend.

Gideon carries Otto with him
everywhere he goes.

Otto likes to be carried.

Gideon swims with Otto.

Otto holds his breath.

Gideon hides with Otto.

Otto peeks out of the leaves.

Gideon reads to Otto.

Otto listens quietly.

Gideon sees two bunnies
playing.

He puts Otto on top of the
stone wall. "Stay here and
don't move," says Gideon.

Gideon dashes off to play.

Otto sits very still.
He quietly waits for Gideon.

Gideon and the bunnies leap over a pumpkin.

"Catch me!" cries Gideon.

Gideon and the bunnies
scamper over the stone wall.

Otto tumbles into the grass.

"Gideon, time for dinner,"
Mama Goose calls.
The bunnies scurry home.

Gideon hops back to find Otto.
Otto is gone.

"Otto, time to go home,"
calls Gideon.

No Otto.

Gideon searches everywhere for Otto.

But no Otto.

Gideon misses Otto.

Then he sees something
slowly moving in the grass.

"Otto!" shouts Gideon.

Otto rides on the back of
a green turtle.

Gideon loves Otto.
Otto loves Gideon.